CAPTAIN UNDERPANTS
AND THE ATTACK
OF THE TALKING TOILETS

CAPTAIN UNDERPANTS AND THE ATTACK OF THE Talking Toilets

TRA-LA-LAAAA

Horizon Elementary School
46665 Broadmore Drive
Sterling VA. 20165

Another Epic Novel by

DAV PILKEY

THE BLUE SKY PRESS
An Imprint of Scholastic Inc. • New York

THE BLUE SKY PRESS

For information regarding permission, please write to:
Permissions Department,
The Blue Sky Press, an imprint of Scholastic Inc.,
555 Broadway, New York, New York 10012.
The Blue Sky Press is a registered trademark of Scholastic Inc.

Library of Congress catalog card number: 98-27382
ISBN 0-590-63136-5
10 9 8 7 6 5 4 3   9/9 0/0 01 02 03

Printed in the United States of America   37
First printing, February 1999

This book has been approved by

P.E.T.T.

People for
the Ethical
Treatment of
Toilets

Free
Newsletter

Free
Membership
Card

To join, send a self-addressed,
stamped, business-sized envelope to:
"People for the Ethical Treatment of Toilets"
c/o The Blue Sky Press
555 Broadway
New York, NY 10012

FOR ALAN BOYKO

CHAPTERS

THE TOP-SECRET TRUTH ABOUT CAPTAIN UNDERPANTS

By George Beard and Harold Hutchins
(who deny everything)

Once upon A Time There were two cool kids named George and Harold

We are cool

me too.

They made Their own comics ABOUT A super Hero named CAPTAIN UNDERPANTS

TRA LA LAAAA

Everybody Thought Thier comics were Funny

HA-HA-HA-HA HA

CAPTAIN UNDERPANTS

CAPTAIN UNDERPF

EXSEPT FOR Thier MEAN old Principel, MR. KRUPP.

BLAh BLAh BLah

CHAPTER 1

GEORGE AND HAROLD

This is George Beard and Harold Hutchins.
George is the kid on the left with the tie
and the flat-top. Harold is the one on the
right with the T-shirt and the bad haircut.
Remember that now.

Depending on who you asked, you'd probably hear a lot of different things about George and Harold.

Their teacher, Ms. Ribble, might say that George and Harold were *disruptive* and *behaviorally challenged*.

Their gym teacher, Mr. Meaner, might add that they were in serious need of a major *attitude adjustment*.

Their principal, Mr. Krupp, would probably have a few more choice words to include, like *sneaky*, and *criminally mischievous*, and *"I'll get those boys if it's the last thing I . . ."* Well, you get the idea.

But if you asked their parents, they'd probably tell you that George and Harold were smart and sweet, and very good-hearted. . . even if they were a bit silly at times.

I'd have to agree with their parents.

But even so, their silliness *did* get them into a lot of trouble, sometimes. In fact, it once got them into so much trouble, they accidentally almost destroyed the whole planet with an army of evil, vicious talking toilets!

But before I can tell you that story, I have to tell you *this* story. . . .

CHAPTER 2

THIS STORY

One fine morning at Jerome Horwitz Elementary School, George and Harold had just gotten out of their fourth-grade remedial gym class when they saw a big sign in the hallway.

It was an announcement for the Second Annual *Invention Convention*.

George and Harold had fond memories of last year's Invention Convention, but this year's convention was a bit different. The first-prize winner got to be "Principal for the Day."

"Wow," said George. "Whoever gets to be principal gets to make up all the rules for the whole day, and everybody in school has to follow those rules!"

"We have *got* to win first prize this year!" exclaimed Harold.

Just then, George and Harold's principal, Mr. Krupp, showed up.

"A-HA!" he shouted. "I'll bet you two
are up to no good!"

"Not really," said George. "We were
just reading about this year's contest."

"Yeah," said Harold. "We're going to
win first prize in the contest and be
Principals for the Day!"

"Ha, ha, ha, ha, ha!" laughed Mr. Krupp. "Do you *honestly* think I'd let you two enter this year's contest after that stunt you pulled at *last* year's Invention Convention?!!?"

George and Harold smiled and thought back to the First Annual Invention Convention. . . .

CHAPTER 3

THE FLASHBACK

It was about one year earlier, and all of the faculty and students of Jerome Horwitz Elementary School had gathered in the gymnasium for what would later be known as the "Sticky Chair Incident." George and Harold stepped up to the microphone.

"Ladies and gentlemen," said George, "Harold and I have invented something that is guaranteed to keep you all *glued to your seats*!"

"Yes," said Harold. "We call it *glue*."

Mr. Krupp became very angry. "You two did not invent *glue*!" he shouted. He stood up to take the microphone away from Harold, and his chair stood up with him. Everyone in the gymnasium laughed.

The school secretary, Miss Anthrope, stood up to help remove Mr. Krupp's chair from his pants. Her chair stood up with her, too. Everyone in the gymnasium laughed harder.

The other teachers stood up, and—
you guessed it—they were stuck to their
chairs as well. Everyone in the audience
howled with laughter.

One kid stood up to go to the bath-
room, and his chair came up with him,
also. The audience stopped laughing so
hard. They all quickly checked their
chairs, and suddenly, the laughter stopped
completely. Everyone in the whole school
was glued to their seats.

You see, while it was true that George and Harold had not invented glue, they *had* invented a new *kind* of glue. By simply mixing rubber cement with concentrated orange juice mix, they had created a quick-drying, body-heat-activated glue. Then they applied this special glue to every seat in the gymnasium (except theirs) early that morning.

Everybody in the gymnasium was glaring at George and Harold and *seething* with anger.

"I've got a good idea," said George.

"What?" asked Harold.

"RUN!!!" cried George.

George and Harold were grinning
from ear to ear, remembering their silly
invention and the chaos that followed.

"That was hilarious," laughed Harold.

"Yeah," chuckled George. "It'll be hard
to top that *this* year!"

"Well, you won't get a chance this year,"
said Mr. Krupp. He took out a magnifying
glass and held it up to the fine print on
the sign.

"This contest is open to all students
in the third and fourth grades EXCEPT
George Beard and Harold Hutchins. . . ."

"You mean, we can't enter the contest?" asked Harold.

"It's worse than that," laughed Mr. Krupp. "You boys can't even *attend* this year's convention. I'm putting you two in study hall that whole day!" Mr. Krupp turned and walked away, laughing victoriously.

"Rats!" said Harold. "What are we going to do now?"

"Well," said George, "you know the old saying: If you can't join 'em, *beat 'em*!"

CHAPTER 4

THE INVENTION

Early that evening, George and Harold
sneaked back to school with their supplies.
They crept into the gymnasium and
peeked around.

"I think somebody's still in here,"
whispered Harold.

"Oh, it's just Melvin Sneedly," said
George.

Melvin was the school brainiac. He was
busy putting some last-minute touches
on his new invention for the contest.

"We should wait here until he leaves," whispered Harold.

"No way," said George. "He could be here all night! Let's just go over and talk to him."

When Melvin saw George and Harold approaching, he was not happy. "Oh, *no!*" he said. "I'll bet you guys are here to mess with everybody's inventions."

"Nice guess," said George. "Listen, we promise not to mess with *your* invention, if you promise not to tell anybody that you saw *us* here tonight."

Melvin looked lovingly at his invention, and reluctantly agreed. "I promise," he said.

ELECTR
APPLE

JTO-
TIC
OE

"Great," said George. "Say, what is that invention of yours, anyway? It just looks like a photocopy machine."

"Well, it *used* to be a photocopy machine," said Melvin, "but I've made some major adjustments to it. Now it is an invention that will revolutionize the world. I call it the PATSY 2000."

"It'll revolutionize the world, and you named it *PATSY*???" asked Harold.

"Yes," said Melvin. "PATSY is an acronym for Photo-Atomic Trans-Somgobulating Yectofantriplutonic-zanziptomiser."

"I'm sorry I asked," said Harold.

PATSY 2000

ATOMIC TEAPOT

"Allow me to demonstrate," said Melvin. "The PATSY 2000 can take any one-dimensional image and create a living, breathing, three-dimensional copy of that image. For example, take this ordinary photograph of a mouse."

Melvin placed the photo of the mouse onto the glass screen of the PATSY 2000 and pressed Start.

The lights in the gymnasium dimmed as all the power in the entire school seemed to get sucked into the PATSY 2000. Soon the machine began to vibrate and hum loudly, and tiny bolts of static electricity snapped out from underneath.

"I hope that thing doesn't explode," said Harold.

"Oh, this is *nothing*," said Melvin. "You should have seen how the PATSY 2000 reacted when I copied a *poodle*!"

Finally, after a series of flashes and loud zaps, everything stopped. A small *ding* was heard, then a tiny mouse crawled out the side door of the PATSY 2000 and onto the floor.

"Isn't it wonderful?" exclaimed Melvin.

George inspected the mouse closely.

"That's a great trick," George laughed. "You really had me goin' for a while!"

"It's *not* a trick," cried Melvin. "The PATSY 2000 really *does* bring photos to life! I've even created living creatures from *paintings and drawings*!"

"Yeah, *right*!" laughed Harold. "And I thought *we* were con artists!"

George and Harold walked away chuckling. It was time to move on to bigger and better things.

CHAPTER 5

BIGGER AND BETTER THINGS

George and Harold went to the other end of the gymnasium, opened their backpacks, and began to work.

George busied himself by turning all the spray nozzles on the *Automatic Dog Washer* around, while Harold filled up the soap tank with India ink.

Then they moved on to the *Volcano Detector*. "Will you please pass me the big bag of butterscotch pudding and a Phillips-head screwdriver?" asked Harold.

"Sure," said George, as he carefully inserted eggs into the *Electric Ping-Pong Ball Server*.

CHAPTER 6

THE INVENTION CONVENTION

The following day started out sunny and cheerful. The students and faculty filed into the gymnasium and checked the seats *very* carefully before sitting down.

"Greetings," said Mr. Krupp, who was standing up at the microphone. "You don't need to worry about sticky seats today," he said. "I've taken measures to ensure that *this* Invention Convention won't be a disaster like *last* year's."

Everyone settled in as Madison
Mancini, a third grader, stepped onstage to
demonstrate her *Automatic Dog Washer*.

"First," said Madison, "you put your dog
in the tub. Then you press this button."

Madison pressed the Start button. At
first, nothing happened. Then suddenly,
a spurt of inky black water sprayed up

and out over the crowd. Everyone (except the dog) got soaked, as Madison tried desperately to turn off the sprayers.

"I can't stop it!" she cried. "Someone turned all the nozzles around!"

"Now *who* could've done that?" asked Mr. Krupp.

Next up was Donny Shoemyer, with his Electric Ping-Pong Ball Server. He turned the machine on, and immediately it began hurling extra-large grade-A eggs into the crowd.

"Phoop!-Phoop!-Phoop!-Phoop!-Phoop!" went the machine.

"Splat!-Splat!-Splat!-Splat!-Splat!" went the eggs.

"I can't turn the machine off!" cried Donny. "Somebody jammed a paper clip into the controller!"

"Now *who* could've done that?" asked Ms. Ribble.

Freddie Moore's Volcano Detector was also a big flop. When Freddie connected the circuits to the nine-volt battery, a large spring (which had been crammed into the center of his miniature volcano) launched a giant plastic bag of butterscotch pudding high into the crowd.

It landed somewhere between the third and fourth rows. *Splat!*

"Hey!" whined Freddie. "Somebody put pudding in my volcano!"

"Now *who* could've done that?" asked Mr. Meaner.

The rest of the day went on much the same way, with people shouting everything from "Hey! Who put oatmeal in my solar-powered leaf blower?" to "Hey, who let all the mice out of my treadmill dune buggy?"

It wasn't long before everyone fled the gymnasium, and the Second Annual Invention Convention had to be called off.

"How could this have happened?!!?" cried Mr. Krupp as he wiped chocolate syrup, pencil shavings, and cream-of-mushroom soup off his face and shirt. "George and Harold have been in study hall all day long! I put them there *myself*!"

"Um, excuse me, Mr. Krupp," said Melvin Sneedly. "I think I have an answer to your question."

CHAPTER 7

BUSTED

CRASH! went the door to the study hall room. Mr. Krupp stomped in like a crazy person. George and Harold had *never* seen him this upset before.

"You boys are in *SO* MUCH TROUBLE!" Mr. Krupp shouted. "I'm putting you two on PERMANENT DETENTION for the REST OF THE SCHOOL YEAR!"

"Wait a second," cried George. "You can't prove anything!"

"Yeah," said Harold. "We've been here all day!"

Mr. Krupp smiled devilishly, and looked toward the door. "Oh, *Melvin*," he called.

Melvin Sneedly stepped into the room, covered in mustard, eggshells, and shredded coconut.

"They did it," Melvin said, pointing at George and Harold. "I saw 'em last night in the gym!"

"Melvin!" cried George, horrified. "You *promised*!"

"I changed my mind," Melvin said, grinning smugly. "Have fun in detention!"

CHAPTER 8

THE INVENTION CONVENTION DETENTION

After school, Mr. Krupp ushered George and Harold into the detention room and wrote a long sentence on the chalkboard.

"From now on," growled Mr. Krupp, "you boys will spend *two hours a day* after school copying this sentence over and over. I want every chalkboard in this room filled *completely*!"

On his way out the door, Mr. Krupp turned and said with an evil grin, "And if either of you leaves this room for *any* reason, I'm going to *suspend* you both!"

Now, as you might have guessed, writing sentences was nothing new to George and Harold. The two boys waited until Mr. Krupp left the room, then they each took four homemade wooden rods out of their backpacks. The rods had holes in them that George and Harold had drilled in George's dad's woodshop.

George screwed the rods together, while Harold inserted a piece of chalk into each hole.

Then they each took a pole and began
copying Mr. Krupp's sentence. Every time
they wrote one sentence, the wooden
poles made twelve!

After about three and a half minutes,
every chalkboard in the room was
completely filled.

George and Harold sat down and admired their work.

"We've got a lot of time on our hands now," said George. "Got any ideas?"

"Let's make a new comic book!" said Harold.

So the two boys took out some paper and pens and created an all-new adventure about their favorite superhero. It was called *Captain Underpants and the Attack of the Talking Toilets*.

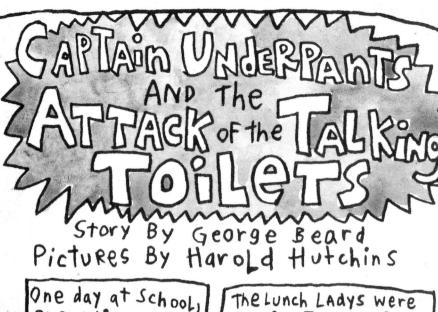

CAPTAIN UNDERPANTS AND THE ATTACK of the TALKING TOILETS

Story By George Beard
Pictures By Harold Hutchins

One day at School, everything was Pretty Normel...

The lunch ladys were serving Toasted Rat Sanwiches...

The Principel was Yelling...

Blah Blah Blah

And The gym Teacher was Being mean to everybody.

My Grandma Can Run Faster Than you guys!

Then a U.F.O. Apeared.

It Zapped The School with a evil Ray.

The ray made all of The Toilets come To Life. It made Them evil, Too.

The Toilets were Hungry.

Yum Yum eat 'em up!

So They ate The gym Teacher.

Help! The Toilets Just Scratched Somebodys Car and ate up The Gym Teacher!

Lord have Mercy! WAS it my CAR?

This looks like a job for... CRASH

CAPTAIN UNDERPANTS

Captain Underpants ran to the storage room.

Yum Yum eat 'em up!

Storage room

He found a bunch of plungers.

He put them in the toilets.

There mouths got stuck.

TRA-LA-LAAA

They had A big Fight.

CAPTain Underpants was Faster Than A Speeding WAiStbAnd...

ZiP

More PowerFuL Than Boxer Shorts...

TRA-LA-LAAA!

Kick

And abeL To Leap TALL BuiLdings WiThout Getting A Wedgie.

CAPTain Underpants Snuck up Behind The Turbo ToiLet 2000, And gave him a wedgie.

Wedgie Power!

Ouchie

CHAPTER 10
A BIG MISTAKE

George and Harold sat together in the detention room, reading through their newest comic book and beaming proudly.

"We've got to go to the office and make copies of this," said George, "so we can sell them on the playground tomorrow."

"We can't," said Harold. "Don't you remember? Mr. Krupp said he'd *suspend* us if he caught us leaving this room!"

"Then we won't let him catch us," said George.

George and Harold sneaked out of the room quietly and crawled down the hall to the office.

"Uh-oh," said Harold. "There's a bunch of teachers in there. We'll never get to use the copy machine."

"Hmmm," said George. "Are there any other copy machines in this school?"

"How about the one that Melvin had in the gym?" asked Harold.

"Oh, yeah," said George.

George and Harold crept over to the gym and found the PATSY 2000.

"I wonder if this machine still makes copies," said Harold. "Melvin *did* say that he had made some adjustments to it."

"Oh, he probably just crammed a mouse in there to fool us," said George. "It's the oldest trick in the book. I'm sure the machine still makes regular copies."

George placed the cover of their new comic book facedown on the glass screen and pressed Start.

All at once, the lights in the whole
school dimmed, and the PATSY 2000
began to shake and clunk around wildly.
Giant volts of static electricity zapped out
the bottom of the machine as a great
whirlwind rose from the top. Loose papers
and other small objects in the room were
sucked into the wind, and they spun above
the machine like a raging cyclone.

"I don't think it's supposed to do this!"
shouted George over the horrible noise.

Finally, after a series of flashes and loud
zaps, the noise, wind, and sparks stopped
altogether. The only sound that could be
heard was of something groaning and
clawing about inside the bloated,
battered frame of the PATSY 2000.

"It sounds like something's *alive* inside
there," said Harold.

George snatched the comic book from
the top of the machine. "Let's get out of
here!" he cried.

Just then, a small *ding* was heard, and a full-sized, shiny white toilet emerged from the side of the PATSY 2000. Its teeth were sharp and jagged, and its angry eyeballs glowed with red, swelling veins. "YUM, YUM, EAT 'EM UP!" cried the evil toilet.

Almost immediately, another talking toilet emerged, followed by another, and another, and *another*. "YUM, YUM, EAT 'EM UP!" they cried.

"Oh, *NO!* Melvin was *RIGHT*!!! The Photo-Atomic Trans-Somgobulating Yectofantriplutoniczanziptomiser really *DOES* create living, breathing, three-dimensional copies of one-dimensional images!" Harold cried convolutedly.

"I've got an idea," said George.

"What?" asked Harold.

"RUN!" cried George.

CHAPTER 11

THE INVENTION CONVENTION DETENTION SUSPENSION

George and Harold screamed and ran out the gym door, closing it tightly behind them.

"A-*HA*!!!" yelled Mr. Krupp, who was just coming down the hall. "You boys left the detention room! You know what that means, don't you?!!?"

"*It wasn't our fault!*" cried Harold.

"*Too* bad!" Mr. Krupp shouted with delight. "You boys are officially *SUSPENDED*!!!"

"Wait," cried George. "You've got to listen! Behind this door is an army of evil, vicious talk—"

"I don't have to listen to you boys *ever again*," laughed Mr. Krupp. "Now get your stuff and get out of this school!"

"But... but...." Harold stammered, "you don't understa—"

"GET OUT!!!" Mr. Krupp screamed.

George and Harold groaned and walked to their lockers to collect their stuff.

"Gosh," said Harold. "In one day we've gotten a detention, a suspension, *and* we've created an army of evil talking toilets who want to take over the world."

"That's a pretty bad day, even by *our* standards," said George.

"Oh, well," said Harold. "I just hope things don't get any worse."

CHAPTER 12

THINGS GET WORSE

Word spread quickly throughout the office that George and Harold had been suspended. The teachers rushed out to cheer and laugh at the two boys.

"You're in big trouble now," chuckled Miss Anthrope. "I can't wait to call your parents and tell them the news!"

"Let's take their desks outside and chop them up!" cried Ms. Ribble.

"Let's throw a party in the gym!" shouted Mr. Meaner.

"*NOOO!*" cried George. "Whatever you do, *DON'T* open the door to the gym!"

"We can do whatever we like," snarled Mr. Meaner as he dashed over to the gymnasium door. "Look, I'm opening the door!" He quickly opened the gym door. "Now I'm closing the door," he said.

"Now I'm opening the door again, and now I'm—*AAAAAAAAHH mmblemble* gluh!"

An evil toilet had stuck its mouth through the door, snapped Mr. Meaner up, and swallowed him whole! *"Flusssssh!"*

The Talking Toilets then pushed their way through the open gymnasium doors and spilled out into the hallway.

"YUM, YUM, EAT 'EM UP!" the toilets bellowed. "YUM, YUM, EAT 'EM UP!"

The teachers couldn't believe their eyes. They screamed and ran for their lives. Only Mr. Krupp, Ms. Ribble, and George and Harold remained, frozen in fear. They watched, paralyzed, as the talking toilets came nearer and nearer. Finally, Ms. Ribble pointed at the toilets and snapped her fingers.

"SNAP!"

"Go away," she cried. "Go away this minute!" But the toilets didn't listen. They moved closer and closer.

66

Finally, Ms. Ribble turned and ran. Mr. Krupp, however, just stood there in a daze. George and Harold looked up at him.

"Uh-oh," said Harold. "Did she just *snap her fingers*?!!?"

"Yep," said George. "Now we're *really* in trouble."

And George was right, for at that moment, Mr. Krupp had begun to change. A silly, heroic smile came over his face as he stood defiantly before his foes.

"I'll put a stop to you vile villains," he said fearlessly. "But first, I need some *supplies*!!!"

Mr. Krupp turned and dashed to his office. George and Harold ran after him.

"Why did Ms. Ribble have to snap her fingers?!!?" cried George. *"Why?!!?"*

"Never mind that," cried George. "Mr. Krupp is turning into Captain Underpants! We've got to pour water over his head before it's too late!"

CHAPTER 13

IT'S TOO LATE!

When George and Harold reached Mr. Krupp's office, they found only his clothes, shoes, and toupee on the floor.

"Look," said Harold. "The window is open, and one of the red curtains is missing."

"What do we do now?" asked George. "Do we save Captain Underpants, or do we stay here and get eaten by a bunch of toilets?"

"Hmmm. . . . Let me think about that one!" said Harold as he climbed out the window.

George quickly collected Mr. Krupp's things and shoved them into his backpack. Then he jumped out the window after Harold. The two boys slid down the flag-pole and ran off after Captain Underpants.

"Where does he think he's going?" asked George.

"I have *no* idea," said Harold. "But we'd better run fast because I think we're being *followed*!"

Captain Underpants dashed through the backyards of some nearby houses and collected pairs of underwear from the clotheslines.

"Mommy," said a little boy looking out his window, "a man in a red cape just stole our underwear."

"And now two boys are being chased
by a ferocious-looking toilet with sharp,
pointy teeth, screaming, 'Yum, yum,
eat 'em up!'"

"Yeah, *right*!" laughed his mother.
"Just how *gullible* do you think I am?!!?"

CHAPTER 14

THE TALKING TOILET TAKEOVER

When Captain Underpants was finished commandeering the underwear of local civilians, he dashed back to Jerome Horwitz Elementary to save the day.

The school was now overrun with chaos. Ms. Ribble came tearing out the door, followed by several evil toilets.

"Help me!" she cried. "They've swallowed every teacher in the whole building except me!"

"Don't worry, ma'am, I won't let them eat you up," Captain Underpants said, as

a toilet ate her up.

"Oops!" said Captain Underpants.

Now, only George, Harold, and Captain Underpants were left. They stood on the front lawn of the school, completely surrounded by hungry, drooling toilets.

"YUM, YUM, EAT 'EM UP!" the Talking Toilets chanted. "YUM, YUM, EAT 'EM UP! *YUM, YUM, EAT 'EM UP!* YUM, YUM, EAT 'EM UP!"

"We're *doomed*!" cried Harold.

"*Never* underestimate the power of underwear!" cried Captain Underpants, as he stretched and shot underwear into the waiting mouths of the Talking Toilets.

Unfortunately, the toilets just swallowed the underwear whole. It only seemed to make them hungrier and hungrier.

"If only we could think of something
that would make them really *sick*,"
said George.

"Yeah," Harold continued. "Something
so vile and disgusting, it would make
them all *blow their cookies* and writhe
in agony!"

Suddenly, George and Harold's faces lit
up. "CAFETERIA FOOD!" they shouted.
And faster than a speeding waistband, our
three heroes dashed into the school.

CHAPTER 15

CREAMED CHIPPED BEEF TO THE RESCUE!

George, Harold, and Captain Underpants got inside the school safely and closed the front door behind them. "I think the toilets are all outside," said George.

"But not for long," said Harold.

Quickly they ran to the school's kitchen and discovered a cart holding a large vat of something green and sludgy.

"Yuck," said George, holding his nose. "What *is* that stuff?"

"I think it's tomorrow's lunch," said Harold.

"Perfect!" said George. "I never thought I'd be *glad* to see creamed chipped beef!"

Together, they wheeled the tub of stinky green glop down the hallway and out the side door of the school. Captain Underpants sat on the cart and stretched a pair of underwear over his head like a slingshot.

George stood over him, scooped some cafeteria food into the underwear, and stretched it back. Harold wheeled the cart toward the Talking Toilets.

"Tra-La-Laaaaaa!!!!" shouted Captain Underpants loudly.

The Talking Toilets turned and saw our three heroes. All at once, they shouted "YUM, YUM, EAT 'EM UP!" and the chase was on!

THOK!

Harold pulled the cart across the playground as the toilets zipped after them.

"Fire One!" cried Captain Underpants.

George shot a glob of creamed chipped
beef into the first toilet's mouth. The toilet
swallowed it whole.

Harold kept pulling, as George scooped
another serving into the underwear and
pulled it back.

"Fire Two!" cried Captain Underpants.

Zip! went the cafeteria food, right into
the *second* toilet's mouth.

The whole process repeated itself until every last toilet had swallowed at least two servings of creamed chipped beef.

"We're almost out of ammo!" Captain Underpants shouted.

"And I don't think I can run anymore," said Harold, huffing and puffing.

"Don't worry. . . *look*!" said George, pointing at the toilets.

They had all slowed down and were beginning to groan and wobble around. Their eyes crossed, and they turned an odd shade of green.

"Look out," cried Harold. "I think they're gonna *hurl*!"

And that's just what they did!

George, Harold, and Captain Underpants watched as the toilets upchucked everything they had eaten during the day. The creamed chipped beef, the underwear, even the teachers all came out without a scratch.

Then the toilets spun around in small circles and fell to the ground, dead.

George checked the teachers. "They're *alive*," he said. "*Unconscious*, but alive!"

"Wow," said Harold. "That was *easy*!"

"*Too* easy," said George.

"What do you mean?" asked Harold.

George pulled their comic book out of his backpack and showed it to Harold. "Remember how the PATSY 2000 turned everything on the front cover of our comic book to life?" he asked.

"Yeah, so?" said Harold.

"Well," said George, as he pointed to the *Turbo Toilet 2000* on the front cover of the comic. "We haven't seen *him* yet!"

CHAPTER 16

THE TURBO TOILET 2000

Suddenly, the Turbo Toilet 2000 came charging out the front door of the school with a terrible *CRASH*! The earth rumbled beneath its mighty footsteps as nearly a ton of twisting steel and raging porcelain descended upon our heroes.

"You three meddling fools *may* have destroyed my army of Talking Toilets..." screamed the Turbo Toilet 2000, "...but you're *all out* of cafeteria food! How are you gonna stop *ME*?!!?"

"I'll tell you how," Captain Underpants said boldly. "With *Wedgie Power*!"

"*Wait*, Captain Underpants!" cried George. "You can't fight that thing! He'll rip you to pieces!"

"Boys," said Captain Underpants nobly, "I *must* fight valiantly for Truth, Justice, and *all* that is Pre-Shrunk and Cottony!"

Captain Underpants leaped onto the Turbo Toilet 2000, and the battle began.

"I sure hope this doesn't lead to extremely graphic violence," said Harold.

"Me, too," said George.

CHAPTER 17

THE EXTREMELY GRAPHIC VIOLENCE CHAPTER, PART 1 (IN FLIP-O-RAMA™)

WARNING:

The following chapter contains intense scenes showing a man in his underwear battling a giant toilet.

Please do not try this at home.

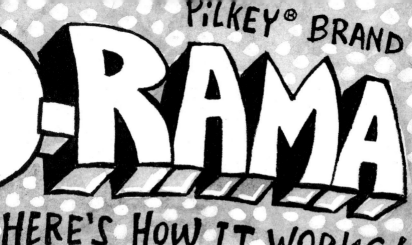

PILKEY® BRAND
-RAMA

HERE'S HOW IT WORKS!

STEP 1
Place your *left* hand inside the dotted lines marked "LEFT HAND HERE." Hold the book open *flat*.

STEP 2
Grasp the *right-hand* page with your right thumb and index finger (inside the dotted lines marked "RIGHT THUMB HERE").

STEP 3
Now *quickly* flip the right-hand page back and forth until the picture appears to be *animated*.

(For extra fun, try adding your own sound-effects!)

FLIP-O-RAMA 1

(pages 93 and 95)

Remember, flip *only* page 93.
While you are flipping, be sure you
can see the picture on page 93
and the one on page 95.
If you flip quickly, the two
pictures will start to look like
one *animated* picture.

Don't forget to
add your own sound-effects!

LEFT HAND HERE

WEDGIE POWER
VS.
POTTY POWER

WEDGIE POWER
VS.
POTTY POWER

FLIP-O-RAMA 2

(pages 97 and 99)

Remember, flip *only* page 97.
While you are flipping, be sure you
can see the picture on page 97
and the one on page 99.
If you flip quickly, the two
pictures will start to look like
one *animated* picture.

Don't forget to
add your own sound-effects!

LEFT HAND HERE

OH, *NO!!!*
THE POTTY POWER
PUNCH PREVAILS!

OH, *NO!!!*
THE POTTY POWER
PUNCH PREVAILS!

FLIP-O-RAMA 3

(pages 101 and 103)

Remember, flip *only* page 101.
While you are flipping, be sure you
can see the picture on page 101
and the one on page 103.
If you flip quickly, the two
pictures will start to look like
one *animated* picture.

Don't forget to
add your own sound-effects!

LEFT HAND HERE

THE CARNIVOROUS COMMODE CAPTURES THE CAPTAIN!

THE CARNIVOROUS
COMMODE CAPTURES
THE CAPTAIN!

CHAPTER 18

HAROLD AND THE PURPLE BALL-POINT PEN

Everything seemed hopeless. Captain Underpants had slipped and fallen into the mouth of the Turbo Toilet 2000, and now the giant toilet was coming after George and Harold!

"Ha, ha, ha, ha, ha!" laughed the powerful porcelain predator. "Once I have eaten you two kids up, I will *take over the world*!"

"Not if *we* have anything to say about it!" yelled George.

George and Harold ran into the school and locked the door behind them. The Turbo Toilet 2000 banged against the door with its fists, shouting, "You boys can't hide in there forever!"

George and Harold ran to the gym.

"I've got a plan," said George. "We need to invent a character who can defeat a giant robot toilet."

"How about a giant robot urinal?" asked Harold. "We can call it *The Urinator*!"

"No way!" said George. "They'll never let us get away with that in a children's book. We're skating on *thin ice* as it is!"

"All right," said Harold, "how about a giant 'Plunger' robot? He can carry a really big plunger, and—"

"That's it!" cried George.

So Harold took out his purple ball-point pen and began to draw.

"Give him *laser* eyes," said George.

"All right," said Harold.

"And give him turbo-atomic rocket boosters," said George.

"Got it," said Harold.

"And make him obey our every command," said George.

"I'm *way* ahead of you," said Harold.

Harold finished his drawing, and George inspected it carefully.

"This just *might* work," said George.

"Yeah," said Harold. "If the PATSY 2000 can hold out."

The boys turned and looked at the dented, cracked, and beaten-up machine laying on its side in the corner. George and Harold pushed the PATSY 2000 upright and dusted it off.

"Come on, PATSY, old girl," said George. "We really need you now!"

"Yeah," said Harold. "The fate of the entire planet is in our hands!"

CHAPTER 19

THE INCREDIBLE ROBO-PLUNGER

George took Harold's picture and placed it on the screen of the PATSY 2000 and pressed Start.

The lights around them dimmed as the weary machine began to shake and smoke. Lightning bolts zapped, thunder clapped, and the whole gymnasium shook with Photo-Atomic Trans-Somgobulatory Yectofantriplutoniczanziptic energy.

"C'mon, PATSY!" George shouted over the horrible noise. "You can do it, baby!"

Finally a small *ding* was heard, and the PATSY 2000 coughed up a huge, metallic behemoth. It rose up and stood valiantly before George and Harold. It was the Incredible *Robo-Plunger*.

"*Hooray!*" cried George. "It *worked*!"

"Way to go, PATSY!" Harold cheered. "Now let's get outside and kick some Turbo Toilet Tushy!"

CHAPTER 20

THE EXTREMELY GRAPHIC VIOLENCE CHAPTER, PART 2 (IN FLIP-O-RAMA™)

NOTICE:

The following chapter contains terribly naughty scenes depicting a giant toilet getting its shiny hiney kicked.

All toilet violence was carefully monitored by P.E.T.T. (People for the Ethical Treatment of Toilets).

No actual toilets were harmed during the making of this chapter.

FLIP-O-RAMA 4

(pages 113 and 115)

Remember, flip *only* page 113.
While you are flipping, be sure you
can see the picture on page 113
and the one on page 115.
If you flip quickly, the two
pictures will start to look like
one *animated* picture.

Don't forget to
add your own sound-effects!

LEFT HAND HERE

THE INCREDIBLE
ROBO-PLUNGER
TO THE RESCUE!

113

RIGHT
THUMB
HERE

THE INCREDIBLE ROBO-PLUNGER TO THE RESCUE!

FLIP-O-RAMA 5

(pages 117 and 119)

Remember, flip *only* page 117.
While you are flipping, be sure you
can see the picture on page 117
and the one on page 119.
If you flip quickly, the two
pictures will start to look like
one *animated* picture.

Don't forget to
add your own sound-effects!

LEFT HAND HERE

THE INCREDIBLE
ROBO-PLUNGER KICKS
THE TT 2000'S TUSHY!

RIGHT
THUMB
HERE

RIGHT
INDEX
FINGER
HERE

THE INCREDIBLE
ROBO-PLUNGER KICKS
THE TT 2000'S TUSHY!

FLIP-O-RAMA 6

(pages 121 and 123)

Remember, flip *only* page 121.
While you are flipping, be sure you
can see the picture on page 121
and the one on page 123.
If you flip quickly, the two
pictures will start to look like
one *animated* picture.

Don't forget to
add your own sound-effects!

LEFT HAND HERE

THE TT 2000 TAKES THE PLUNGE!

121

RIGHT
THUMB
HERE

122

THE TT 2000
TAKES
THE PLUNGE!

CHAPTER 21

THE AFTERMATH

The Incredible Robo-Plunger had defeated
the evil Turbo Toilet 2000, but George and
Harold's problems weren't over yet. They
reached into the crumpled mouth of the
TT 2000 and pulled out their principal.

"What happened here?" cried Mr.
Krupp. "The school has been *destroyed*,
the teachers are all *unconscious*, and I'm
standing here in my *underwear*!"

"Uh-oh!" Harold whispered. "Captain Underpants must have gotten toilet water on his head. He's turned back into Principal Krupp!"

George took Mr. Krupp's clothes and hair out of his backpack and handed them to him.

"I'm ruined!" Principal Krupp whined as he dressed himself. "I'm going to be held responsible for this mess! I'm going to lose my job!"

"Maybe not," said George. "We can fix everything, and clean up this whole mess."

"Yeah," said Harold, "but it'll cost you!"

"Cost me *what*?" asked Mr. Krupp.

"Well," said George, "we'd like you to cancel our detention *and* our suspension!"

"And we'd also like to be *Principals for the Day*!" said Harold.

"All right," said Mr. Krupp. "If you can really fix *everything*, you've got a deal!"

George and Harold turned and spoke to the Incredible Robo-Plunger.

"All right, robot guy," said George, "make yourself useful and pick up all this mess!"

"Yeah, and fix up the school, too," said Harold. "Use your laser eyes to repair all the broken windows and stuff!"

"And when you're done," said George, "take all the evidence, and fly it up to Uranus."

"And don't come back!" said Harold.

CHAPTER 22

TO MAKE A LONG STORY SHORT

The robot obeyed.

CHAPTER 23

AFTER THE AFTERMATH

The Incredible Robo-Plunger soared off into space just as the teachers began to regain consciousness.

"I just had the strangest dream," said Ms. Ribble. "It was all about these evil toilets who wanted to take over the world."

"We had the same dream, too," said the other teachers.

"Well," said Mr. Krupp, "things turned out all right after all!"

"Not quite," said George. "It's *payback* time!"

CHAPTER 24

PRINCIPALS FOR THE DAY

(OR, THE INVENTION CONVENTION DETENTION SUSPENSION PREVENTION)

"Attention, students," said George over the intercom the following day. "This is Principal George. You are all excused from classes today. There will be no homework or tests, and everybody gets an *A+* for the day."

"That's right," said Principal Harold. "Also, we are hosting an all-day recess outside, complete with free pizza, French fries, cotton candy, and a live DJ. Now go outside and play."

Principal George and Principal Harold strolled out to the playground to behold their glorious domain. George got a slice of pepperoni pizza, while Harold made himself a banana split at the all-you-can-eat ice-cream sundae bar.

"It's *good* to be the principal!" said George.

"Yep," said Harold. "I wish we could be principals every day!"

Later, George and Harold paid a visit to the unfortunate folks who were spending the day writing sentences in the detention room. All the teachers were there, along with Mr. Krupp and Melvin Sneedly.

Mr. Krupp looked out the window at the all-day recess celebration going on outside.

"How are you boys going to *pay* for all that ice cream and pizza?" he asked.

"Oh, we sold some stuff," said Harold.

"What did you sell?" asked Mr. Krupp.

"Your antique walnut desk and leather chair," said George. "And all the furniture in the teachers' lounge."

"WHAT?!!?" screamed Mr. Krupp.

"Umm . . . I think we'd better leave now," said Harold.

George and Harold left the detention room in a hurry. Miss Anthrope snapped her fingers at them.

Snap!

"Come back here right now!" she yelled.

"Uh-oh," said George. "Did Miss Anthrope just *snap her fingers*?"

Within seconds, Mr. Krupp dashed out of the detention room and ran down the hallway toward his office. He had a goofy, heroic, *all-too-familiar-looking* smile on his face.

"Oh, no!" cried Harold.
"Here we go *again*!" said George.

ABOUT THE AUTHOR

When Dav Pilkey was a kid, his teachers thought
he was disruptive, "behaviorally challenged," and
in serious need of a major attitude adjustment.

When he wasn't writing sentences in the
detention room, he could usually be found
sitting at his private desk out in the hallway.
There he spent his time writing and drawing
his own original comic books about a superhero
named Captain Underpants.

It was always Dav's dream to publish a book
about Captain Underpants.
Now that dream has come true . . . twice!

Visit Dav Pilkey's Extra-Crunchy
Web Site O' Fun at:
www.pilkey.com

OTHER COOL BOOKS BY DAV PILKEY

The Adventures of Captain Underpants

Dog Breath

The Hallo-Wiener

The Paperboy

Dogzilla

Kat Kong

The Dumb Bunnies

Make Way for Dumb Bunnies

The Dumb Bunnies' Easter

The Dumb Bunnies Go to the Zoo

'Twas the Night Before Thanksgiving

A Friend for Dragon

Dragon Gets By

Dragon's Fat Cat

Dragon's Halloween

Dragon's Merry Christmas

The Moonglow Roll-O-Rama

The Silly Gooses

When Cats Dream

World War Won

god bless the gargoyles

COMING SOON:
*Captain Underpants and the Invasion of the Incredibly
Naughty Cafeteria Ladies From Outer Space
(and the Equally Evil Lunchroom Zombie Nerds)*